The Glass House Children of Ravenshire
The Forgotten

R.L. Caudill

R.L. CAUDILL

The Glass House Children of Ravenshire *The Forgotten* Copyright © 2013 R.L. Caudill

Published by Full Moon Publishing, LLC
Glade Spring, VA
Website: www.fullmoonpublishingllc.com

ISBN: 0615894712
ISBN-13: 978-0615894713

Edited by Jamie White and CP Bialois
Beta Reader MD Martin

Cover photo purchased from Shutterstock

R.L. CAUDILL

Dedication
To my wonderful family whose love and support
inspire me. I love you Ricky, Brittany, Nikita
and Travis. Special thanks to Nikita for the
expertise on dinosaurs.

R.L. CAUDILL

Chapter 1

In the town of Ravenshire lived an unusual and unique family. Though this was the Frye family, all of the townspeople called the children of this family the Glass House Children. Let me explain. Their house had so many windows held together with gleaming copper that glowed in the sunlight it gave a shiny appearance of being entirely made up of glass.

The Frye children lived in their own fairy tale land. They had many, many adventures. And the best thing about all of their adventures were they never had to leave their own land to set out on a quest—sometimes they never even had to leave their glass house.

Their father jokingly, but not really kidding, would say, "Children who live in glass houses shouldn't throw stones, so be good."

There were five Frye children, two boys and three girls. The oldest child was seventeen-year-old Wesley. He had wavy, chestnut-colored hair, deep brown eyes, and stood tall with a medium muscular build. From an early age, he told everyone he met that he wanted to be a pirate. Wesley spent many hours gaining an abundance of knowledge of the waters, myths about the waters, and creatures that inhabited the fathomless oceans, seas, and lakes. He collected much of his information from Sailor Slim Robins.

Wesley's large bedroom overlooked the vast, calm, azure ocean; sparkling, white lines crested and colossal waves that broke against the rocky cliff base. He often dreamt of mermaids, the lock ness monster, and other sea creatures. His grandmother said it was because the ocean was calling to him and when he became a man, the ocean would be where he must go.

Wesley's room reflected the pull the ocean had upon him. The room was large and filled with murals of seascapes on his walls and skies painted on his ceilings. There was even a mural of a distant lighthouse. Sometimes at night Wesley could swear that he could see the lighthouse beacon flashing.

These murals seemed so real to him, perhaps because they were of his own hands and his own imagination. He painted them all; only he painted in this room. His room was filled with figurines of sea creatures, lighthouses, ships, and other sea-related objects.

He even had an authentic periscope. It was an antique that his grandmother had given him. She said it once belonged to the dread pirate, Black Bellamy.

Wesley's wooden bed was in the shape of a ship with a canopy of billowing white sails and a flag hung above it with the words, "The Mermaid's Delight" upon it.

Being sixteen, James was the second oldest of the Frye children. James' unruly, fiery red locks framed his freckled face while his emerald eyes danced brightly when the sun reflected its brilliance in them. He also had the same build and stature as his older brother.

James' dream was to be an archeologist. He was knowledgeable about gemstones, fossils, mummies, ancient ruins, ancient cultures, and the Earth itself.

James also had a large bedroom, however, it overlooked the lush, grassy front yard. From his room, he could see large boulders protruding through the ground like some giant from below had given them a heave and pushed them upwards.

James' bedroom walls also had murals painted on them depicting ancient places such as Stonehenge, the pyramids of Egypt, the Mayan ruins, and the grand temples of Greece and Rome.

His grandmother told him he was destined to be a traveler and visit those places some day. He had many books of interest. He was a most dedicated scholar of archeology, and had read his entire library with great enthusiasm.

Like his brother, James also had many artifacts. Some of his finds would put the most affluent museums to shame. Some items he found in his own yard, while others were gifts from friends and relatives. They brought those wondrous objects to him from their adventures around the world.

An aunt on his mother's side once brought him a sparkling golden dagger encrusted with rubies, emeralds, and diamonds that had belonged to an Egyptian queen, possibly to Queen Cleopatra. That dagger was his prize procession

His father had built his bed to resemble an Egyptian throne, complete with a gold leaf overlay. It was never duplicated and is still one of a kind.

Trinity was the middle child at age fifteen. Her long blond waves flowed like a golden river as her crystal-blue eyes peaked out from under her wispy bangs. She was of average build for a child her age. The day Trinity was born Ma Frye placed her safely in her crib only to return moments later with a barrage of animals surrounding her. It was no surprise that Trinity dreamt of being an animal tamer and had extensive knowledge of the animal kingdom, both wild and tame.

Trinity also had a large bedroom. Her room overlooked the west side of the forest of towering birch, maple, and pine trees. In the treetops were perched many ebony ravens keeping watch over the Frye land. From her windows she could see the forest animals scurry about, doing their day-to-day things. She loved to sit in her window sill for hours upon end just watching the animals. She loved them all.

Trinity had a menagerie of pets that ranged from cats and dogs to birds and horses. The murals on her wall were of course depictions of animals, both exotic and domestic. She had an affinity with animals. She could approach any animal and because of her respect for them, they did not fear her. Trinity's grandmother declared the day Trinity was born that she would some day be a great animal doctor.

Her bed looked like a mammoth cushion, like something a cat or a dog would sleep on. Upon the downy cushion-like mattress were a multitude of pillows.

Trinity would fantasize about being any animal just before she slept and would dream that she was that particular animal. She would be enlightened as to what it was to be the animal.

Belle, who was the fourth child and fourteen, had beautiful long, black curly locks that constantly kissed her face and flowed down her back like an obsidian waterfall. Her eyes were as black as her hair—so black that her pupils were undistinguishable from the iris. Her skin was pale with rosy cheeks and lips.

Belle's bedroom matched her siblings and overlooked the forest on the east side of the glasshouse. From her room, she could see a variety of beautiful trees and a myriad of plants. The murals that adorned her walls were marvelous lifelike nature scenes containing trees, plants, and flowers.

Belle's ceiling was painted black with white stars so that she could pretend she was sleeping outside. Her bed lay directly on the ground, but it was shaped like a simple wooden box that held her feather mattress. It was covered with a plethora of cozy, handmade blankets and pillows.

Belle loved nature and believed that through nature anything was possible. She had learned many important things from her grandmother, such as concoctions out of herbs that could heal, cause love, relieve pain, etc. Grandma Frye presented Belle with a small crate filled with beautiful colorful bottles adorned with swirls of silver hugging them and corks crowning the tops. She informed Belle that these were for holding potions.

Belle's grandmother also gave her instruction on healing with crystals. Belle could recognize every plant and gemstone, and what they were used for and where they were found.

Belle's grandmother was certain that when Belle reached adulthood she would be a great healer.

Maggie was the baby of the Frye family at only thirteen. She was very petite child. Her hair was light brown with red highlights in it that glimmered in the sunshine. Maggie was blessed with gray eyes.

Now the reason I say blessed is because her gray eyes were special as they could change colors. They would change from gray to blue to green. They changed depending upon the color she was wearing or the mood she was in. However, there was yet another reason that her eyes were special.

Maggie could see and speak to fantastical creatures such as fairies, sprites, brownies, elves, gnomes, and so on. Her grandmother said that Maggie was, and would always be, a fairy charmer. These creatures would help her to be a seer.

Ma and Pa Frye were very special parents. They did not believe in "spare the rod and spoil the child." You see, they wanted children so badly that when they were blessed with each and every child, they knew that for their children to be special they must treat them with great love and respect. They knew that if they did this, then the Glass House Children would be wonderful and very special children.

Ma and Pa Frye owned hundreds of acres of land. They owned almost half of Ravenshire. Ma Frye, Ruby Jean Thompson, was an only child and her family owned many, many acres of land that adjoined Pa Frye's family's land. Now Pa Frye, Earnest Frye, was also an only child. So it was only natural that all that land went to them when they married.

Everyone in Ravenshire knew that Ruby and Ernest were destined to be together forever. Everyone in town knew they had loved each other since they were children.

Ma Frye was a little bitty woman, built much like Maggie. Most of her own children were taller than her by the time they reached the age of twelve. They were all at least as tall as she was by the time they reached the age of ten.

She had long brown hair and kept it flying loose, not even pulling it back even when she cooked. Ma Frye was a free spirit and believed her hair should be free as well. Pa Frye always said her hair was her crown and glory. It hung all the way down to her knees and was beautiful. It looked like a big brown lion's mane. It was silky and shiny and always free.

Her eyes were like Maggie's; they were also gray. They too changed colors and she could see fantastical woodland creatures.

In fact, many times she would tell the children of hearth brownies that helped her to keep their home so clean and beautiful. It didn't matter what kind of clutter was in the glass house, when the children awoke in the morning, the house was spotless. Even all of the huge glass windows would sparkle in the morning sun.

Every night Ma Frye would leave two small bowls out in the living room on the fireplace hearth. One had milk in it and the other had little bits of cake. She would also close the doors to the room to keep the cats and dogs from harming the brownies while they ate or from stealing their food. She would also leave buttons or little scraps of cloth, thread, and gemstones or anything she thought the brownies might like or be able to use.

There was never a night that she did not do this. Even when she was sick, she would make sure that the brownies were cared for.

Ma Frye also always wore beautiful flowing clothing. If she was seen from a distance, one might think that they were seeing a fairy with clipped wings.

Ma Frye was always kind with her looks, her actions, and her words. She could always pick out the good in people and leave out the bad. She did the same with daily situations. She always looked for the good and left the bad.

Pa Frye was tall and with a slim build. He had green eyes and brown hair. He was a kind man.

Pa Frye was never cross with the children and listened to what they had to say. He was always interested and engaged in the conversation of their choice and seemed to know a little about whatever they wanted to talk about.

Pa Frye was a smart man and the children were amazed because he seemed to know something about everything. One last thing about Pa Frye was that he loved Ma Frye endlessly and Ma Frye loved Pa Frye endlessly.

The Fryes never seemed to want for anything. They lived in harmony with nature and seemed to have whatever they needed. They lived off their land and bartered in town for goods that they didn't produce themselves. They were also blessed with a small gold mine on their land where the Frye's and the Thompson's properties met.

Ma Frye always said that it was fate; that her and Pa Frye were meant to be together. She also said that the fairies, elves, brownies, and other fantastical creatures blessed them with that gold mine.

Ma Frye believed this blessing was because the Fryes chose to live in harmony with nature and not just taking from the land and never giving back.

When the Fryes took wild herbs, they left a small stone, seeds, or planted something in its place. When they took a tree, they planted three seedlings in its place. As far as the gold mine, they didn't mine it all. They only took exactly what they needed and left a small basket of fruit, scraps of cloth, or something to show their thanks and respect to the gold mine. Pa Frye also planted several fruit trees around the mine so as to give back to nature.

The Fryes also took in animals that were orphaned or injured. When they were well enough to be on their own, they were set free. Usually the animals stayed on the Frye land and the children would often see them when they were on their adventures.

Grandmother Frye was Earnest's mother. She, too, was sort of a seer. She knew the destiny of each Frye child, and she was correct in her prophecy of each. She was always kind and never had harsh words for anyone.

Grandmother Frye always said that if you had nothing good to say about someone, then don't say anything. She believed that whatever you did came back to you three-fold, especially with actions and words. She believed in reaping what you sow and doted over the children.

Both Frye parents and Grandmother Frye treated the children with great respect, love, and kindness. No matter what they were doing, if the children had something to say, they would stop to listen and engage in a delightful and enlightened conversation with the children. The siblings were in turn respectful and loving toward their elders. They were also respectful to everyone in their community. They were indeed very unique children.

Chapter 2

One beautiful summer day Wesley went into town to work for Becky Bingham on the schoolhouse. She had asked Wesley if he cared to help her move her desk and the bookshelves. He agreed and was happy to help.

After he had finished helping Becky, he walked over to the pub to listen to Slim Robins tell a story or two. Slim had lots of sea stories to tell and Wesley never tired of hearing them. He bound through the door of the pub and hopped up on a bar stool like he was about to order a tall cold one. But instead of ordering a drink he ordered up a story. "Hey ya, Slim, have you got a story for me today?"

"Sure thing, Wesley, I always have a good story. Let me see now," Slim said as he rolled his eyes back in his head like he was searching for one in his brain and rubbed his chin between his index finger and thumb. "Oh yeah, I have just the story for you."

Slim began his story with, "You see now, Wesley, there is a strange world unto itself hidden behind the Ravenshire Cliff Waterfalls. Did you know that? There are plants and creatures that have not been seen by the eye of the common man in so long that they had come to be thought of as myth and legend."

Slim took a deep breath and continued his story, "Once, long ago, the caves had been open and accessible to the townspeople of Ravenshire. The townspeople had become jealous and greedy and developed impure hearts. The townspeople exploited and took advantage of these creatures and all that they had to offer. The creatures became exceedingly unhappy and fearful of humans, so they prayed to the Nature Goddess for help.

"The creatures wanted to be hidden, protected, and forgotten by the rest of the world. The goddess answered their prayers and came in the form of a massive giant storm that Ravenshire had never seen the likes before, nor have they since. This storm ravaged the land and the ocean alike. It was so strong that it pushed into the side of the mountain under the cliffs a large hole. This hole formed caves that extended deep into the mountain of Ravenshire, leaving exposed only a cliff and the Ravenshire Cliff Waterfalls.

"There was no easy access to the caves. In fact, they weren't even visible. These caves were hidden, along with the creatures, behind a beautiful curtain of flowing, white water. These creatures were thankful that their prayers were answered and that their goddess had taken pity upon them and had hidden them from the rest of the world. They never again came out into the open and were eventually forgotten by man except in the form of legend, which no one believed," Slim finished his tale with a smile.

Wesley sat there wide-eyed pondering how he might make his way behind those falls.

Slim leaned onto the counter and asked Wesley, "What did you think of that one? Do you think there really are mythical creatures and a hidden world behind the falls?"

Wesley did believe. After all, he knew there were hearth brownies and fairies so why would it be impossible for other such creatures to exist? He also believed that he would one day find them. Now he dreamt of exploring the caves.

Wesley shook his head and replied, "I do. But, Slim, how do you know all of this?"

"Let's just say I have been around and have heard a lot."

Wesley asked, "Do you believe the story?"

"Of course I do. I have seen too many things not to believe this, too, is possible." Slim smiled and continued, "Well, Wesley, I have talked long enough. I must get back to work. But you come back in a day or two and I will see if I can remember another story for you."

"Thanks, Slim, I will." Wesley sauntered back out and on home, all the way pondering over how he could get behind that waterfall.

Now since there was no way to enter the caves other than from the cliff face, he decided that what he needed was a ship to sail there and then he would be able to go behind the falls and explore the deepest depths of those caves. However, Wesley didn't just want any ship, he wanted an airship.

He hurried home and went to his father and said, "Pa, I want to build an airship, but I need your help. Will you help me?"

"Pray tell, why on earth would you want to build an airship?"

"Well, I went by to see Slim and he told me that there was a hidden world behind the Ravenshire Cliff Falls. I want to explore them."

Pa Frye agreed. "Yes, I will help you. But you will have to responsible for most of the work."

"Of course, Pa. I just need you to give me instruction and help with what I can't do alone," Wesley replied.

Pa told Wesley that they would begin the next morning right after breakfast. Wesley was excited; after his maiden voyage to the falls maybe he would take Emilia McMurray, the merchant's daughter, back for a picnic.

At supper that evening Wesley informed the rest of his family about the airship and the falls. His siblings and mother offered to help as well.

That night Wesley couldn't get to sleep no matter how hard he tried. He was so excited about having a ship of his own.

Finally, Wesley dozed off. However, he felt he had not closed his eyes long before the cock was crowing for him to rise and shine. Despite being sleepy, he was excited and jumped from his bed and grabbed his work clothes. He dressed in such a hurry that he forgot to put on his socks. He got half way to the kitchen before he realized it and had to go back up and finish dressing his feet.

He finally made his way to the kitchen and gobbled down his breakfast so fast he had to wait on his father to finish his.

Ma Frye scolded him, saying, "Wesley, you shouldn't eat so fast. It will give you the vapors and you will not be a pleasure at all to work with."

Wesley coaxed his father to hurry. Pa Frye finally finished his breakfast and they headed to the work shed together. Wesley knew his father had eaten slower than usual just to make him wait.

Wesley walked down to the work shed with his father. "Okay, Pa, where shall we begin? Let's get started."

Pa Frye wasn't a hurrying man. He warned Wesley not to get into a rush. "If you don't take your time and make sure that you do things right, then you're just wasting your time. Anything that is worth doing is worth doing right. And doing it right means taking your time and checking everything twice."

Wesley, like all the Frye children, learned lessons well and remembered what they had learned. He took a minute for reflection. He thought about his pa's words of wisdom and the time that he had built a birdhouse.

Wesley had hurried through its planning and construction. The finished product was very weak. He hung it in a tree near the house so that he could watch the birds fly in and out, perch, and eat. Before any little birds could make a home in it, a strong breeze blew it apart.

"Wesley," Pa Frye had said that day, "anything that's worth doing is worth doing right. Doing it right means taking your time and checking it twice."

In remembering that time with the birdhouse, the lesson he had learned and the wise words from his father, he decided to try and contain his excitement. He would slow down and concentrate on the task at hand rather than the adventures that he would have once his ship was complete. So he gathered his thoughts and listened very carefully to everything that Pa Frye had to say. He watched intently and learned a few things. They began by drawing up building plans for the airship that included sails, propellers, and the same glass and copper that adorned their house.

It wasn't long before the entire family had made their way to the work shed. The Frye family worked for a good month solid. Finally, with much hard work from all Frye family members, the airship was complete and ready for her maiden voyage.

It was the end of summer and school was scheduled to begin in a week. A trip to the falls just before school began was a perfect way to end summer vacation.

The vessel had billowing, white sails draped from a wooden frame and a carving of a mermaid keeping watch at the bow. The name of the airship painted on both sides was *The Mermaid's Delight*.

Wesley was extremely proud of The Mermaid's Delight. He stood back and reveled in the sheer beauty of its stunning wooden hull, the flowing sails, massive patchwork silk balloon, and the monumental copper propellers mounted to the front and the back of the imposing ship.

Wesley couldn't wait to take The Mermaid's Delight out for her maiden voyage. The anticipation of venturing out to the Ravenshire Cliff Waterfalls, cascading down from the precipice into the ocean was almost more than Wesley could bear.

He asked his father if he could take The Mermaid's Delight out the next day to the caves behind Ravenshire Cliff Waterfalls and his father agreed.

Wesley needed a crew to help him man The Mermaid's Delight, as he knew he couldn't do it alone. So he asked his siblings if they would like to be his crew. When he told the other children of his plans to visit the caves, they were all very excited and eager to go with Wesley on this adventure.

Wesley was already seventeen and almost a man. After all, Pa Frye had been just a few months older than him when he married and began his family. When the other children asked if they could accompany Wesley, the Frye parents approved. The only stipulations were that Wesley insured the safety of his siblings and that they be home by sundown.

The children hugged and thanked their parents and began to ready themselves for the journey. Maggie, Trinity, and Belle packed food and drink, extra clothes, and bedding. The extra clothes and bedding were just in case of an emergency. Wesley and James packed the survival gear and first aid supplies. All of the Frye children went to the vessel and stored their supplies.

After they had readied the ship for their journey, the children retired early that night so as to be rested for their adventure. They awoke with the cock's crow and dressed in clothing appropriate for an adventure. The girls opted for tan safari slacks and white cotton shirts instead of their three-quarter length flowing dresses that they typically wore. Instead of their dainty shoes, they wore knee high leather boots. They all braided their hair and banded the braids with thin leather strips. The boys also wore their safari pants with white cotton shirts and black leather boots.

The children went to the kitchen where they were greeted by their parents and grandmother. The Frye family ate an enjoyable breakfast of gravy, biscuits, eggs, bacon, and fruit together. Afterwards, the Glass House Children and their parents made their way to The Mermaid's Delight for departure.

The dirigible hovered silently above the dock awaiting her maiden voyage. Its sides gleamed in the predawn light with The Mermaid's Delight emblazoned in beautiful gold script. At the bow, the figurehead of a mermaid with flowing locks proudly met the blush of first light as the Glass House Children waited patiently for their send-off.

The children all stood at attention as Pa Frye inspected their gear for the voyage. He nodded his approval as he inspected the ship, assured they had both necessities and emergency provisions.

When Pa Frye had concluded his inspection of the ship, Ma Frye smiled brightly as she inspected the children. She straightened shirts and tucked away an errant lock of hair then nodded her approval as well.

Finally, their grandmother eyed them up and down then gave a final nod as she handed a heavy basket to Belle. Belle peeked inside to find fruit, meat, and fresh-baked bread along with a large glass jar of water.

After the inspection was complete their father, mother, and grandmother hugged the children as they boarded the vessel one by one. The first child to set foot aboard was Wesley. Wesley helped Maggie, Trinity, and Belle to board The Mermaid's Delight from the ship and

James helped the girls from land. James was the last to board. They put on their brass-trimmed goggles to protect their eyes and were ready to embark.

The Frye children could barely contain their excitement. They were, however, responsible children and knew that they must conduct a safety check. Everyone had jobs to do. When they had taken care of all that was needed, they raised the sails, turned the helm and set off for adventure. They didn't need to plot a course; they knew exactly where their destination lye.

Chapter 3

The Ravenshire Cliff Waterfalls were just a few miles north of where The Mermaid's Delight had been docked. The caves were on the outskirts of the Frye land. The Frye children were not certain if the extent of the caves continued on their land or if the caves encroached on some neighbor's property. They didn't know if the caves went deep into the ground with only one entrance or if the caves stayed relatively close to the surface with other openings.

As they drifted on the trade winds they each exchanged tales of their ideas and what they thought would be found in the caves.

Wesley was the first to share his thoughts. "I bet we find buried treasure that was stashed away by some poor, unfortunate pirate. We may even find his bleached bones. And I'm sure we will find the hidden creatures that Slim told me about."

Maggie had other ideas. Even though she was the youngest on this adventure, her thoughts were still revered by the other children.

"I bet there are strange mythological creatures living in the caves," she replied, enjoying the discussion.

Since Maggie was a seer from a very young age, the other children knew she must be correct. Yet they still gave their own theories about what was to be discovered in those caves.

"I think we will find new plants that can cure diseases. Wouldn't that be a wonderful discovery?" Belle added to the speculations.

All the children agreed that it would be exciting to find plants that could cure mankind's ills.

"I'm going to find extinct animals. We might even find pre-historic ones, but if we do we should not reveal them. We should protect them and make sure they are safe from mankind," Trinity said after a moment of silence.

James was certain that each Glass House Child would find something exciting. "I'm sure we will all learn something valuable and take important knowledge away with us at the journey's end. However, I know I'm going to discover some important, forgotten and valuable archeological finds."

He proclaimed to the other children, "I will discover relics from the fairy folk who took refuge here so long ago. Like Trinity, I wouldn't reveal my discoveries to the rest of the world. The townspeople didn't respect the beings before who took refuge in the Ravenshire Caves. How could we trust then to respect them now?"

The Glass House Children thought long and hard about the points that Trinity and James had brought up. They continued to exchange ideas and theories of what they would find in the caves. Time passed quickly while they worked industriously.

Maggie suddenly squealed out with great excitement, making the other children jump. They turned from their tasks to see what she was going on about and their mouths dropped open as they saw a wondrous sight—The Ravenshire Cliff Waterfalls loomed up before them. The runoff from a nearby river—the Ravenshire River—that created the falls flowed from the top of the cliff like white, silk curtains blowing in the wind. Hidden behind those curtains of water were caves that went back into the side of the cliff face. The cave entrance was hidden behind the falls but Wesley knew where to find it. He knew this because Old Slim Robins had told him.

On further examination of the area, various kinds of birds and butterflies flew close to the beautiful white curtain of water and the surrounding land. Birds of many colors circled and dove, riding the thermals. There were blue, white, red, yellow, orange, black, and purple birds. Trinity recognized some, but there were others that she had never seen or heard of before.

Trinity suddenly pointed. "Look, look! Do you see those purple birds? I have never seen anything like them before! And the butterflies, those with the pink and yellow swirls on their wings, I don't know what they are either!"

Maggie began to jump up and down and yelled excitedly, "Hurry, Hurry!"

"We have all day, and we now have The Mermaid's Delight and can come back anytime. We could come back every day if we want to," Wesley assured her.

"Really?" Maggie whooped while jumping up and down.

Belle, who had been struck speechless by the wondrous sight, simply uttered, "Wow."

James was certain after seeing the falls that there must surely be archeological marvels hidden within the caves hidden behind that majestic, white curtain never before seen by human eyes.

"I just know that there are marvelous relics inside those caverns. There has to be," he proclaimed, his eyes shining brightly at the prospect.

Wesley turned the ship toward the shoreline. They all pitched in and in a combined effort, brought The Mermaid's Delight to the seashore, hovering whimsically above the sparkling waves crashing against the shoreline. They dropped the anchor deep into the water to keep the magnificent flying ship from floating away in the trade winds. Wesley threw the rope ladder down across the side of the tiny ship. They all climbed down the ladder with Wesley once again in the front and James staying behind to help. They descended The Mermaid's Delight one by one until all were safely on land.

They took their backpacks filled with supplies and began their ascension up the cliff side. Now you might think that the cliff side would be all rocky, but it wasn't. It was somewhat rocky, but there were also other obstacles. Trees, roots, grass, shrubs, and other types of foliage on the embankment leading up the side of the cliff made their climbing slow and treacherous.

Many trees stood at attention, embellished with fairy holes in their bases. The small holes at the base of the trees appeared to be naturally carved. The holes had raised ridges around them where the tree had healed itself; this is where fairies live.

Maggie was ecstatic to see the fairy holes. She was very experienced in spotting fairy holes, since she visited the fairies around the glass house daily.

Maggie squealed out with excitement, "Look, I knew it. I told you there would be fairies here! I told you! I know they are hiding. Can't we please stop, just for a minute, and let me coax them out?"

"We can't stop yet," Wesley replied. "This is our first trip. I assure you that we will come back again.

Besides how many fairies have you encountered at home everyday? How many?"

"A lot, every day," she said with a pout because she knew that her brother was right.

"Come on, now!" Wesley exclaimed, "Let's see what's behind the falls."

Maggie gave a little smile and replied, "Okay, let's go then."

The others were also eager to enter the caves to see what they would find. They couldn't wait and sprinted up the cliff so fast they appeared to float. But of course that was impossible, right?

As they ascended the cliff side, Belle took notice of plants that were unfamiliar to her. There were beautiful flowering plants that had a wondrous sweet scent. They smelled like a cross between roses and orange blossoms. She breathed deeply, taking in the intoxicating, sweet aroma. She didn't ever want that scent to disappear. She noticed that the other children were also sniffing that same beautiful bouquet. As they ascended further up the cliff side the scent did not diminish nor fade, it only became stronger.

The higher they climbed, the more exquisite things they found. Exotic fruits they had never before seen or tasted hung in abundance from the tree branches. They wanted so badly to try them, but erred on the side of caution instead. They did not take the risk, even though they really wanted to.

When they finally made their way to the entrance of the caves, they found that it was wet and slippery. Wesley made them all hold hands as he led the way and James stayed behind as an anchor.

Maggie turned to look at a beautiful pink and purple bird that was dipping in and out of the waterfall when she lost her footing and, loosing her grip on James, slid down the side of the cliff. The chain reaction also brought Belle over the side and Trinity half hanging over the edge on her stomach holding on dearly to Belle who was, in turn, grasping Maggie.

Wesley held tight to Trinity as he wedged his feet against a nearby boulder. Clinging to the cliff side, James made his way to Trinity and pulled at her until she was no longer half dangling over the edge. Finally, Wesley, James, and Trinity had enough leverage to pull Belle, and then Maggie, to safety. They all sat looking at one another in relief, disbelief, and terror after realizing what a close call they had just encountered.

After regaining composure, the children carefully made their way behind the waterfall curtains and into the caves. They stood in utter amazement at what their eyes beheld.

The children were surprised to find the cave walls illuminated. They gave off so much light that the inside of the caves were as bright as the sunlit outside. They expected it to be dark and creepy, but it wasn't. It was beautifully lit and very inviting.

"Wow!" Belle exclaimed. "But how is it so bright?"

James was taken aback by its beauty, but it was no enigma to him and he explained to Belle and the others. "It's the fluorite."

Now Maggie, being inquisitive, promptly asked, "What is fluorite?"

"It's a thermo luminescent rock. So when it gets hot, it glows and gives light," James replied.

"What's making it hot?" Belle asked.

James' brow furrowed. "I'm not sure."

Wesley looked around at the beautiful water trickling down the cave walls and on the farthest wall there was another huge waterfall. He hadn't noticed it before because of the sound of the falls at the cave entrance.

None of them had noticed the second waterfall because they were so caught up in their initial impression of the cave.

Wesley was the first to approach the second waterfall. He slowly extended his hand and let the water flow across his fingers.

"It's warm," he mused then turned to the others and smiled brightly. "The water's warm."

James had an epiphany. "That's it!"

"What's it?" asked Wesley with his hand still in the warm trickling water.

"That's why the fluorite is glowing. There must be hot springs somewhere feeding warm water to these caves."

They surveyed the cave. Belle spotted more strange looking fruits in the trees. The trees had huge and thick dark foliage hanging from the branches. The fruit on the branches looked like a cross between a melon and an orange.

"How do these plants grow in the warm water?" she asked as she wandered over and touched the strange fruit. She was surprised that the fruit was fuzzy like a peach.

"Well," James replied, "the water must cool as it runs down the cave walls and by the time it gets to the plant roots it's tempered by the chill of the rock. If you'll notice here, the fluorite at the bottom of the walls doesn't glow as brightly as it does near the top."

James crouched down and let the water in one of the natural drainage trenches run through his splayed fingers. It led away from the walls to a larger stream.

"Yep," James confirmed, "It's cool and the stream is getting larger. There must be a place in these caves where all this water empties out, like an underground river or something,"

"Let's follow the river," exclaimed Belle, "I want to see what other kinds of plants there are in here."

Maggie squealed with delight. "Oh! Oh! Did you see that? It was over there where we came in, at the 'tween place, at the entrance of the cave."

Maggie was a very special child and could see 'tween places, which are doorways between realms where humans live and the realm of magic. It is a doorway where fairies and other magical creatures can enter and exit the human world.

"What was it?" Belle's voice was a gentle balm inside the cave.

Maggie replied excitedly, "Over there! Over there! Didn't you see it?"

"I don't see anything," Belle answered.

The other children chimed in unison. "I didn't see anything either."

"What was it?" Wesley asked.

"It was fairy folk. They were over there where we came in, at the 'tween place," Maggie insisted, pointing excitedly.

Maggie had the gift of sight since she could remember and she had seen many fantastical creatures, but she had never seen fairies like these before.

"Look, there they are again! Look! Don't you see them?" she pleaded.

"No," the other children replied.

"What do they look like?" Trinity asked.

"There is a girl and her mama. The girl has long, curly black hair and a pink dress that looks like it is woven from spider webs. She has pink and yellow wings. Her mama has long, curly black hair and purple and pink wings. The mama's dress is yellow and looks like it is woven from spider webs too. Oh, please tell me that one of you can see them," she begged.

"We can't, I'm sorry," Wesley apologized.

"Wait a minute," Maggie said, "They want me."

"Be careful, Maggie," Belle warned.

"Oh, they won't hurt me. They want to tell me something. I have to get close, their voices are tiny and hard to hear," Maggie said over her shoulder as she approached the 'tween place. She leaned over and appeared to be speaking to thin air. She leaned closer as if she were listening very hard.

Finally, claps her hands, "Yes that would be great! Thank you! Thank you!"

"What? What?" Belle asked.

"Just wait a minute. You'll see," Maggie replied as she stretched out her hands, palms up towards the 'tween place.

"What are you doing?" Wesley asked in wonder.

"Just wait." Maggie's tone had grown a little annoyed by all the questions.

Maggie said thank you to the invisible beings then joined her siblings, still holding her hands out in front of her.

The other Glass House Children looked at each other in bewilderment. Maggie blew something from her open palms into the other children's faces.

"Hey! What are you doing? What was that?" they all yelled while rubbing their eyes.

They blinked several times as if they were trying to clear sand from their eyes and after a few minutes, their vision cleared. They looked at Maggie and to their amazement, hovering in the air close to Maggie's face, they saw the fairy folk.

Trinity was the first to speak. "How can we see them? We don't have the gift of sight."

"You do now, at least while you're in the caves," Maggie boasted, pleased with herself by being able to prove to the others that she had made such a significant discovery. "The fairies gave me fairy dust from their wings. When it was blown into your eyes it opened them to seeing all kinds of fantastical creatures, including fairies."

Trinity replied, "But we didn't see anything in your hands."

Maggie beamed. "Of course not, silly. It was fairy dust. You couldn't see the fairy folk or the fairy dust until the dust was blown into your eyes to open them up to the fairy world. Look at your hands and at each other. You all look so funny."

They all looked down at their hands and then at each other. They began to laugh uncontrollably.

"You look so funny. So do you. You all do," the children said to one another. They were all covered with a rainbow of colored fairy dust.

The Glass House Children could all now see the fairy dust that coated their hands and hair and had settled on their clothes. They rinsed their hands and faces in the warm waterfall.

They were all very excited to go forward and encounter their next discovery. Maggie walked back over to the 'tween place and asked the fairies if they could be the children's guides. The fairies felt the children were friendly and would do them no harm, so they agreed to this. They hadn't seen humans in hundreds of years and they were excited to spend time with the children and ask them questions about the human civilization. Trinity asked the fairies what their names were.

The mother said, "My name is Floranna and my daughter's name is Rosella. What are your names?"

Maggie introduced the Glass House Children to the fairy folk. "I am Maggie. These are my sisters, Belle and Trinity, and these are my brothers, Wesley and James."

"Where did you come from? We haven't seen humans for hundreds of years," asked Floranna.

"We're from Ravenshire. We're the Frye children. Actually, these caves are on our land and protected by our family. We don't allow hunting and our land is completely fenced in to protect it from outsiders. We have no trespassers on our land," Wesley said.

"There are rarely ever any strangers that come to Ravenshire at all. The people of Ravenshire very rarely go to the outside world. In fact, most people who were born in Ravenshire have never ventured outside the perimeter of our town. We keep to ourselves. Our town is very happy with our way of life and don't wish to bring the outside world into ours," explained Wesley.

"Interesting," said Floranna as she flitted in the air. Then she asked, "Shall we proceed forward?"

"Sure," the children replied.

Chapter 4

Wesley cautioned the fairies about venturing too far. Wesley explained about the promise that they had made to their parents, so they could only explore for a little while longer. Floranna said that she understood and explained that their fairy village wasn't far.

Once they proceeded, Maggie began to bombard the fairies with questions. "So why did your kind and others who dwell here cut yourselves off from humans?"

Floranna answered, "Probably for much of the same reasons that your town has cut itself off from the outside world. We didn't want human influence in our way of life and we became fearful of them."

Floranna began to tell the Glass House Children of how, long ago, fairies and humans lived in harmony with one another, the animals, and the other fantastical creatures. Eventually humans began to show greed and jealousy. They wanted all that was theirs and all that the fantastical creatures had to offer as well. One by one, each of the different types of fantastical creatures stopped interacting with the humans. The humans hunted them for what they could give.

They prayed to the goddess of nature to hide them from the humans. She hid them in the caves, making them almost completely inaccessible to humans. The goddess knew that the humans were lazy and they would not go to the trouble of climbing the cliff side and venturing deep into the caves to find them.

Wesley recognized this as the same story Slim had told him in the pub.

"But how did you live among the humans if they couldn't see you? Did you dust everyone's eyes with fairy dust?" Maggie asked.

"Oh no, the humans could see us before," Rosella chimed in, "The Nature Goddess feared that one day humans might find the caves, so she gave us the gift of invisibility. Only the righteous and honest ones can see us, only the ones who are truly pure at heart. All children can see us, but when they get older they become blind to us. You all have seen fairies when you were very young, you just don't remember. Only a few keep their gift of sight past the age of six or seven."

Maggie interjected, "That's what my mother and grandmother say that I have. They, too, have it. We see fairies and other fantastical creatures where we live."

Rosella exclaimed, "There are those of us who still live among humans? We thought that we, the ones who live in the caves, were the only ones left."

"No," said Trinity. "Our mother says we have hearth brownies that live in our house and there are fairies who live in fairy holes in our trees."

"Have you seen them before?" Rosella asked.

"No," Trinity replied, her face drooping. "I have not. Only Maggie, our mother and grandmother have seen them. They are the only ones with the gift of sight."

"Tell us, Maggie, who are these fairies and hearth brownies? Where did they come from? Why are they still living among humans?" Floranna asked.

Maggie replied, "Well, you see, the hearth brownies still help our family. They help our mother with household chores at night when we are all sleeping. Our mother always leaves them food and other goods. They stay inside our house and made their homes inside the walls."

Wesley chimed in, "Our mother says there are many hearth brownies living in our home. She has told us the names of some. The eldest of them is Brybuckle. He says he was a small brownie when the others left and his clan decided to stay. There were a few others who stayed with our family."

Maggie took the conversation back by saying, "There are still fairies living among us. I speak with them everyday. They help us to bring in good crops each year. Some of the fairies are Lavina, an elder, and Karnish, her mate. There are also sprites that live among us. But we have never seen a sylph or an elf."

Rosella said, "There are sylphs that live among us, but no elves."

Belle said, "I am fascinated with the phoenix. Have you ever seen one?"

"Yes," Rosella said, "There is a phoenix that visits us once in thirteen moons."

"Why only once in such a time?" questioned Wesley.

"I am not certain. It has always been this way. If we need him sooner, all we have to do is call to the goddess for help and she will send him. The Nature Goddess has put us in his charge. He is our guardian protector," replied Floranna.

The Glass House Children and the fairies continued on their journey into the caves while they continued to exchange information about the other's way of life, their history, their families, and their friends.

The further into the caves they traveled the more strange the plants and animals became. The Frye children saw all of these strange plants that had never before been seen by human eyes. They saw flowers as tall as they were.

There were fruits hanging in the trees as large as the children's heads. These fruits looked sort of like giant strawberries, but more rounded and they were purple. They were the deepest, darkest purple the children had ever seen before.

The Glass House Children saw birds flying around in the caves, some of these birds were as big as small calves. The children were utterly amazed. The birds consisted of a myriad of colors.

The children were getting tired and hungry. Though they were excited about all the wonders they were encountering, they knew they must stop to eat and rest. They asked the fairies if that would be all right and the fairies agreed.

The children started to get their food and drinks from their knapsacks, but their new friends coaxed them into eating some of the purple fruit. The fairies called it sranna, which kind of resembled a large, pink banana.

They stopped at a huge mushroom patch and ate their sranna. They all leaned up against the huge mushrooms and enjoyed this new fruit, which when peeled back was pink and tasted like a mixture of banana and strawberry.

"This is amazing!" James exclaimed and all of the children liked the new fruit. Now the mushrooms they sat under were the size of a huge oak tree that grew outside in front of the Glass House Children's home and resembled huge multicolored umbrellas. Eating under the huge mushroom reminded the children of picnics they had during the summer months with their parents.

The mushroom patch was enormous. Some mushrooms had swirled designs, some had circular designs, and some had designs similar to that of a butterfly's wings.

Once the tuckered out children had eaten and rested, they were ready to continue on their journey. The children and their guides hadn't ventured very far before they came upon vast beautiful meadows. They gazed upon the tall grass as it blew back and forth in a light breeze. Where this breeze came from, the children did not know.

Beautiful wild flowers grew in abundance. Some of the flowers were small but, again, most were oversized. They were anxious to see what lye around the next corner.

"Where are all of the other creatures, Floranna?" Maggie asked.

"They remain hidden deep within the caves. Not many of us ever venture to the cave's entrance," Floranna replied.

The children and the fairies continued their journey deeper and deeper into the caves when suddenly they heard a terrible screeching. It was the squawking of a phoenix as it flew past them so fast that the wind blew their hair back. It flew toward the center of the caves in the same direction as the children and the fairies were headed.

"Oh no!" Rosella cried.

"What?" the children exclaimed in unison.

"It's the phoenix! There must be trouble in the village!" Floranna replied. "Come children, we must hurry."

Chapter 5

They ran as fast as they could, following the fairies deeper into the caves and occasionally stumbling on rocks. As they neared the center of the caves where the fairy village lay, they heard screams and a terrible roaring and growling. They couldn't believe what they saw.

"Oh my goddess, how can this be?" Floranna cried out.

As they came into viewing distance, they could see the destruction was massive. Huge, ugly, scary creatures terrorized the village. These creatures were very large—about twice the size of a grizzly bear with long dirty claws and sharp yellow fangs. They had green, bulging eyes and lumpy brown skin.

The children were horrified. They had never seen anything like that before in their lives.

"What are those things?" Belle asked, trying to swallow her fear.

"They are trolls," cried Rosella.

"Quickly! We must hide in these trees!" Floranna shooed them urgently towards the lower branches of some of the nearby tree trunks.

They all climbed as quickly as they could. The girls went first with the boys helping to give them a boost.

When they were safely hidden within the branches of the trees with their little fairy friends beside them, Wesley whispered, "What do we do? Where are the other fairies—the other creatures?"

"They must have gone into hiding. We need to find them. The phoenix was still squawking and flying about as if he were calling out to the fairies."

"What is the phoenix looking for?" Trinity asked.

"He is looking for fairies in need of help. If he sees any, he will rescue them. If he doesn't see any, he will fly back to the Nature Goddess and let her know what has happened," Floranna explained.

"What can we do to help?" James asked.

"Nothing, we wait," Floranna replied.

"We can't just sit and wait. We have to do something," Maggie's urgent whisper was met with a grim shake of Floranna's head as the phoenix flew back past the children and the fairies.

"So the other fairies must be safe, right? The phoenix didn't rescue any. So now he is going to get the Nature Goddess?" Maggie asked.

69

"Well, there must not have been any fairies or other creatures that needed to be rescued, but that does not mean that everyone is well," Floranna replied.

"You mean some could be dead?" Tears welled in Maggie's eyes and spilled down her cheeks.

"That is possible, but let's hope for the best, shall we?" Floranna replied as she touched one of the tiny tears that spilled from Maggie's eyes.

"These things are really trolls?" James asked, hating to see his sister so distraught.

"Yes, but we haven't seen any since the Nature Goddess brought us here to keep us safe. The trolls are very dangerous. They respect nothing. They are ruthless and kill just for the sake of killing. So the Nature Goddess left them above ground with the humans. The trolls found their own hiding places from the humans— under bridges," Floranna explained.

70

"We have never seen them before. We had heard about trolls living under bridges and thought they were just stories to scare children into behaving," Trinity said.

"Oh no, they are very real and very dangerous. You would do well to remember this when you return home. Do not linger near bridges and always stay away from their lairs beneath them," Rosella warned.

"We plan on it," Wesley said, "but we really need to find out where they found a way into the caves. Maybe we can force them back out and seal the entrance," Wesley suggested.

"Wesley is right. We need to get the trolls out of here fast," James agreed.

"Ma, we really need to do something. We can't just wait," Rosella begged.

"We shouldn't. We should stay where we are," Floranna cautioned.

"Stay here how long—until they find us?" James asked with a quiver in his voice.

Floranna flew back and forth amongst the branches, careful not to be spotted by the trolls, while rubbing her chin and running her fingers through her hair in frustration. She knew the children had a point. The children and Rosella could tell Floranna was on the brink of agreeing with them. Finally, Floranna nodded in agreement.

"Okay, but you have to follow my instructions— no questions. Agreed?" Floranna said sternly.

In unison, all the children and Rosella said, "Yes, Ma'am."

"Okay. You children must stay here with Rosella until I see if I can find where the trolls came in. Okay?"

"Yes, ma'am, but how long must we wait? What if you find yourself in trouble? How will we know if you need help?" Wesley asked.

"Don't worry, if I need you I will send you a sign." Floranna replied then flew away, stealthily avoiding the trolls.

The children and Rosella did as they were told and waited.

Chapter 6

Floranna fluttered quickly and carefully from tree to tree to avoid being spotted by the trolls. Since trolls have a terrible odor, all she had to do was follow the stench and she would eventually find where they had entered the caves. It didn't take long.

"Humans," Floranna said to herself and flew back to the children.

"I found where the trolls entered," she told them solemnly.

"Where?" Wesley asked.

Maggie could tell something was wrong with Floranna. She could see the sadness in the fairy's eyes. "What is it, Floranna? Something is wrong."

"Humans are the reason the trolls were able to gain access to these protected caves," Floranna replied, her voice a thick mixture of anger and sadness.

"But how? You said they were hidden and inaccessible," Belle asked.

"They were supposed to be, but it looks like humans have been digging down into the ground right above the caves in a thin area of earth. The trolls must have found the hole," Floranna replied.

"That's terrible. Who would be digging and why?" Maggie fought her own tears of frustration that someone had tampered with this majestic world within a world.

"I don't know, but we need to get the trolls out of the caves and find a way to seal the entrance," James declared.

"Well, I know a giant who can seal the entrance with a huge boulder," Maggie replied, remembering one of her friends, "But how do we get the trolls out?"

"How do we get the trolls out? How do you get your giant here?" Belle asked, trying to staunch the incredulous notion that they could accomplish either action.

"I have my ways. But we have to be above ground for her to hear my call," Maggie said, pleased that she could contribute in a giant way.

"Now back to my question, how do we get the trolls out?" Belle asked again.

"I don't think that will be a problem," Rosella replied as she pointed at the phoenix that was once again flying through the caves.

The phoenix landed majestically on a tree limb beside Trinity.

"Well hello there," Trinity said as she stroked his beautiful plumage.

The phoenix cooed as Trinity stroked him.

"We will have help from the Nature Goddess soon," Floranna smiled.

The children nodded, they had always been taught to be patient. Grandmother Frye always said, *"Patience is a virtue,"* and the children wanted to be virtuous. They were also taught to mind their elders, but they were finding it difficult to just sit and wait even though they knew how important patience was and how important it was to do as an elder- instructed. Since Floranna was an adult fairy and probably several hundred years old, she was definitely an elder.

All the same, they sat and waited until they heard a thundering of which they had never heard before in their lives. The children had heard loud thunder crashes from terrible thunderstorms. They had heard the roar of trains. But this was a sound that they did not know.

The children turned and were utterly amazed at what their little eyes beheld. It was a herd of dinosaurs. They were not carnivores—not the T-rex nor Spinosaurus. The dinosaurs that were bombarding their way to the village were a herd of Apatosaurus.

The children clung tightly to the tree so as not to fall. The dinosaurs were so large and there were so many that the ground trembled like a huge earthquake was about to open up a chasm and swallow everything in the cave.

Floranna and Rosella didn't seem as surprised as the children were when the dinosaurs threw their large necks around knocking the trolls up against the cave walls and trampled them under their feet. The trolls that weren't killed by the dinosaurs were forced toward the hole that Floranna had discovered.

The children watched in wide-eyed wonder. How could there be dinosaurs still alive and here in the caves? This was impossible, but there they were trampling the trolls. The children watched on as fear and surprise turned into amazement.

"Okay children, let's go. Maggie, I hope your giant friend comes right away. We are going to need her—and soon," Floranna said as she coaxed the children down from the tree they had been hiding in.

"Oh, she will come. I just need to be above ground," Maggie assured Floranna.

They followed closely behind the dinosaurs—but not close enough to be trampled. The Apatosaurus' forced the trolls back out of the hole.

Floranna flew to one of the Apatosaurus' and whispered in his ear. The dinosaur gave a strange, low growl and lowered his tail and raised his head high—high enough to reach the top of the hole.

"Hop on children we are going above ground," Floranna directed.

"What? Are you sure it's safe? They are massive," James said.

"Oh, dear boy, you have nothing to worry about. The Nature Goddess sent these beautiful beasts to help us. I asked him if he could help us out and he agreed. These are friendly beasts. They will be careful. Now hop on," Floranna instructed.

The children reluctantly did as they were told. They stepped up on the dinosaur's tail and climbed carefully up his scaly, lumpy back and onto his head.

Then they stepped out onto the ground into fresh air and sunshine.

Floranna and Rosella looked around as they blinked their eyes and adjusted to the bright sunlight. The little fairies immediately noticed the lush, green meadow that was blanketed with beautiful wild flowers that gave off an intoxicating, sweet scent.

"Oh, Ma, it's unbelievable up here. I wish we could stay and explore," Rosella almost begged her mother for something she knew was impossible.

"I'm so sorry, my little flower, but we can't. It is not safe. We must go back down to the caves as soon as possible," Floranna replied, her voice filled with regret. She would desperately love to stay above ground and explore longer.

"You can explore close by until the time comes to retreat back to the security of our caves." Floranna smiled indulgently at her daughter as she brushed a wisp of hair from Rosella's eyes.

As the children looked around they recognized the meadow they were in—it was their meadow.

"This is our meadow, but who could have dug this hole and why did they do it?" the children wondered aloud.

"Look, there are the trolls! They are still running," James pointed at them.

Floranna quickly responded, "This is true, but they won't stay away very long. Maggie, you must call your friend."

Maggie pulled a small whistle from under her bodice. It that was dangling from a thin piece of rope and was the smallest whistle the other children had ever seen. Maggie blew hard on it, but they could not hear anything.

"Maggie, your whistle is broken. What will we do now?" Belle asked.

"Silly, my whistle isn't broken. It is so loud that we can't hear it, but my giant friend can."

The words had no sooner fallen from Maggie's lips when the ground began to tremble and they heard a far away *thud, thud, thud.*

Rosella flew quickly back to the others, "I have found something strange in these bushes, come quickly and tell me what it is!"

They all followed Rosella back to the underbrush.

"There, what is that thing?" she asked, pointing at the wood and metal object.

This was something that the children did recognize. The long wooden handle had been the cause of many blisters on the tiny hands of each Frye child. But something strange they did notice was a price sticker that was still on the handle. The shovel and the sticker were from the mercantile.

Trinity also noticed something odd. "Hey, look. Is that what I think it is?"

"You bet. It is a frog trappin' box," James replied as he tapped his foot in disapproval.

"We all know who has been here and who dug that hole," Belle said.

"Rosten!" the other children declared in unison.

"You know the person who dug this hole? But why?" Rosella asked.

"Rosten likes to play tricks on people. Undoubtedly this was one of his tricks. I'm not sure what kind, but it can't be good," Wesley said in dismay. Frustrated as he ran fingers through his hair, "We will find out as soon as we get back home. I promise."

It wasn't long before the thuds became louder. Maggie's giant friend was getting closer with every thud. The other children had never before seen Maggie's giant friend. They had only heard Maggie talk about the giant to their parents.

The giant was a beautiful young girl with long blonde locks and blue eyes. She had rosy cheeks and lips and stood almost 20 feet tall.

Maggie smiled brightly at the sight of her friend bounding her way toward them. The giant girl was laughing as she joined Maggie and the other children.

"Hello, Maggie," the giant's voice thundered. When she spoke, it created a strong breeze that blew everyone's hair and clothing.

"Hi, Genevieve! I am so happy to see you. Thank you so much for coming. We desperately need your help," Maggie said as she and the others looked in the direction of the gapping hole in the ground.

"That hole over there needs a boulder placed across it. The trolls found their way into the fairy caves and they must be blocked out. Can you help us?" Maggie asked, pointing toward the hole.

"Yes, Maggie, I would be happy to help you," the giant girl thundered as she skipped toward a nearby boulder, making the ground shake so hard that the children popped up and down.

She picked up the boulder like she was picking up a pebble. Genevieve carried the boulder over to the hole.

"Now?" she asked as she began to bend over to plug the gapping hole in the ground.

"No. Not yet," Maggie said. "We have to go back down, so we can travel back to The Mermaid's Delight."

The children and the fairies quickly made their way back down the hole and onto the dinosaur's head.

"Okay," Maggie yelled back up to Genevieve, "You can cover the hole. I will call you soon. Thank you, Genevieve. Thank you so much."

Genevieve slowly covered the hole with the boulder as if she were placing a tiny bird back in its nest. As the children and the fairies watched the outside light fade away, they knew that the fairies were once again safely hidden in the caves. They climbed back down the back of the dinosaur.

Chapter 7

Maggie looked around with her lips snarled up in disgust and said, "What will you do with all of the dead trolls?"

Floranna smiled with a twinkle of secrecy in her eyes as she said, "We have fairy dust and you can do many things with fairy dust."

She and Rosella reached into the little pouches that were hanging from a small hemp rope around their necks.

"How?" James asked as he looked around at the corpses of the trolls that littered the fairy village.

James tried to imagine what it had looked like before the devastation of the trolls had occurred.

"Just watch." Rosella giggled as she began to fly around from one troll to another, dusting them with her rainbow-colored fairy dust.

The children were speechless when they saw what began to happen. Right before their eyes, the bodies of the trolls were transformed into lush green grass with beautiful flowers of every color sprouting up from it.

Then huge mushrooms, bushes and fruit trees began to spring up. The fruit trees blossomed and almost immediately had fruit on them.

"Wow," Belle said in wonderment. "That's amazing. What else can fairy dust do?"

Floranna replied as she continued to work on restoring the fairy village, "Well, it can do almost anything. Watch this."

Floranna sprinkled some of the dust on a demolished cottage and it began to rebuild itself. The thatched roof was once again covering the tiny cottage with the veranda once more hugging the sides of the cottage. And beautiful flowers and vines embraced the railing of the veranda and clung to the side of the cottage.

Before long the entire village was as it had been before the trolls came. As the dinosaurs left, they were very careful not to crush the village. The other fantastical creatures cautiously made their way out of hiding and back into the fairy village.

The children had had a long day and were exhausted.

"We should really be leaving," Wesley said.

With looks of disappointment on the faces of his siblings, they all agreed.

"We don't want our parents to be worried and we do want to be allowed to come back. That is, if you don't mind," James said.

"Of course we don't mind, but it is getting late. Will you make it back to your home in time?" Floranna asked as her tiny brows furrowed with concern.

"I'm not sure. I do hope so," Wesley said as he wrung his hands and fidgeted a bit.

The little fairy could tell he was a little nervous about not making it home on time, so she offered a little fairy help.

"With a little dust I can have you back on your vessel. Would you like me to do that?"

"That would be wonderful. I know we can make it home easily from The Mermaid's Delight," Wesley said as a huge smile covered his face.

Floranna and Rosella sprinkled fairy dust over the children's heads as they flitted around.

"Off you go now, back to your vessel—The Mermaid's Delight," Floranna said as the children began to fade from sight.

The two little fairies could hear the faint echo of "Thank you."

Chapter 8

They landed softly on their feet, once again on The Mermaid's Delight. They made haste in getting the airship under way, laughing and talking excitedly about the adventure they had just had. Before long they were back at the small dock they had built just for The Mermaid's Delight. They anchored the dirigible and raced up the hillside and back to the security of their glass house.

They ran into the house forgetting their manners—talking loudly inside, not closing the front door behind them, and not taking their shoes off at the front door.

"Ma, Pa, Grandmother Frye!" they all called out in unison.

As soon as their parents rounded the corner of the foyer, they quickly minded their manners. Wesley closed the front door, they quieted their voices and they kicked off their shoes.

"Well, did you have a good adventure? Was it all you had hoped for?" Pa asked as he opened his arms wide and motioned for the children to come over and give him a hug.

They hugged their pa, then their ma, and then they hugged their grandmother.

"It was amazing," Maggie began as she popped up and down like she had swallowed a handful of jumping beans.

"Oh my, I bet you did have some fun," their mother said as she lightly brushed fairy dust from

Maggie's hair and shoulders, "So come and tell us all about it."

They all went into the living room and excitedly took turns telling their parents about their grand adventure. They also told them about the discovery they had made in the meadow. Pa Frye said he would take care of that first thing in the morning.

"Well since you have all had such a grand adventure, I doubt any of you will have any problems getting to sleep tonight." Ma smiled as she kissed each Frye child lightly on the head.

"Make sure to wash off that fairy dust," Grandmother Frye chortled as they all trooped up the stairs to find their way to bed.

Ma Frye was right; it didn't take any of the children long to drift off and dream about the wonders they had seen.

The next morning Pa Frye went out to the meadow and collected the shovel and the frog trappin' box. He took it straight into town to Mr. McMurray.

Now it took a lot to get Pa Frye upset, and this wasn't one of those times. He explained to Mr. McMurray what Rosten had done and gave the shovel and the frog trappin' box to Mr. McMurray. Pa Frye left the rest up to him.

As Pa Frye left, the mild-mannered Mr. McMurray blew his top. The entire town heard what type of punishment Rosten had received that day. First Mr. McMurray gave him a good old-fashioned thrashing and Mrs. McMurray gave Rosten the talking-to that made you wish you were getting a good old-fashioned thrashing.

As for the Glass House Children—you'll never believe what their next adventure was.

THE FORGOTTEN

Author Bio

R.L. Caudill was born and raised in a small rural town in southern Virginia. She married her high school sweetheart and has two beautiful daughters. She loves everything pertaining to fantasy and fantastical creatures. R.L. Caudill earned a doctorate from Capella University in 2009. She has written several books in other genres.

THE FORGOTTEN